For Antonia and Daniel
A.F.

For Sylvia
K.L.

One day, long, long ago when the world was new,
Lindiwe looked down from the heavens.
She was proud of the universe.
She was proud of the moon and the stars,
the sun and the rain clouds.
But most of all, Lindiwe was proud
of the Earth and all its creatures.
"The world is young and I must make sure
that all is well with it," she said.

Lindiwe called her daughter, Thandi.
"Come, let us take a journey. Let us make sure that
the Earth and its animals are happy."
So it was that Lindiwe and Thandi
came down from the sky.

They strode across the Earth,
over snowy peaks and deep valleys.
They soared with the eagles and danced with the bears.
They marched across forests and grasslands.
They swam with the fish and ran with the deer.

Finally, they came to rest on a vast plain.
There they stood, watching the animals in the distance.
Lindiwe was pleased with the world and its creatures.

But as the sun rose,
they saw that something was not quite right.
Lindiwe was puzzled.
"Why are the trees wilting?" she murmured.
"Why is the soil so dusty?" Thandi asked.
"Why do the animals look so sad?"

Lindiwe and Thandi stood and watched and
thought about these questions.

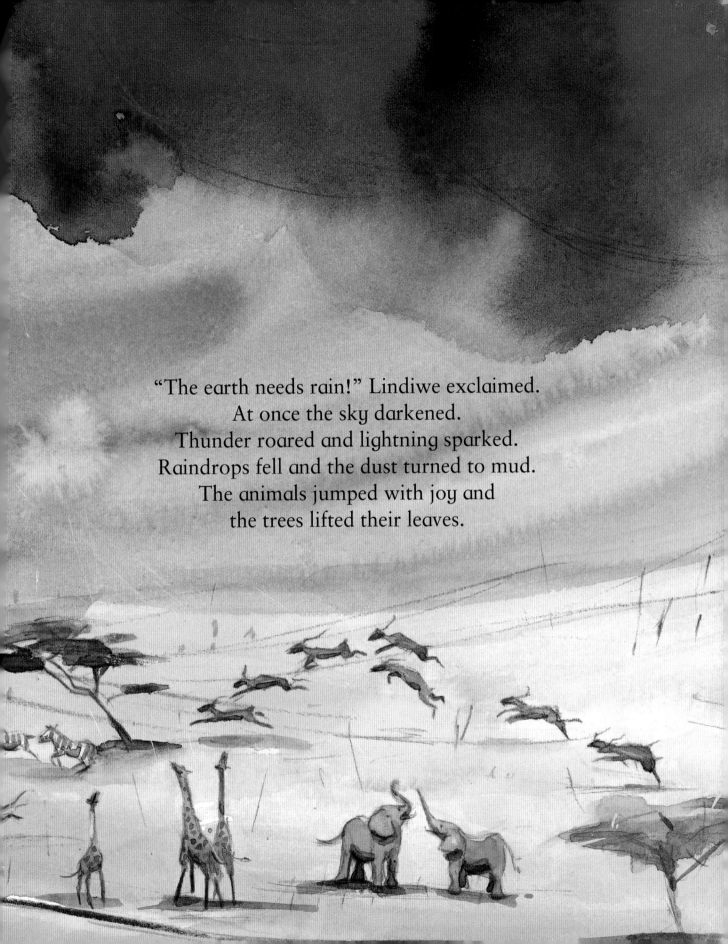

"The earth needs rain!" Lindiwe exclaimed.
At once the sky darkened.
Thunder roared and lightning sparked.
Raindrops fell and the dust turned to mud.
The animals jumped with joy and
the trees lifted their leaves.

Lindiwe was not done yet.
"We need to collect the water," she said.
She gathered a handful of clay and
began to rub it between her palms.
She kneaded and pounded, pushed and pulled.
She turned the clay into a coil, turning it round and round.

She quickly made pots of all shapes and sizes.
Fingers of lightning baked the pots dry.

Thandi collected some bits of clay
that fell from her mother's hands.
She rolled them between the palms of her hands.
"I will make beads from these scraps!" she said.

She strung the beads together and
tied them around her neck.
Then she made her way to the animals.
"Look!" Thandi called.
"Look what I have made!
Lion, you have your mane.
Giraffe, you have your patches.
Now I have these beads!"
"How clever you are," said Lion warmly.

Meanwhile, Lindiwe strode across the land
pushing the enormous pots into the earth.

Water collected in them and
the animals came from far and wide to drink.

Lindiwe spoke to the animals.
"From this day on, when it rains
my pots will fill with water and
you will never go thirsty again."

The animals were overjoyed and wanted
to thank her in a special way.

"Thandi," growled Lion.
"To thank your mother and you,
we will make your necklace as colourful as we are."
Puzzled, Thandi gave her necklace to Lion.
He divided the beads among the animals.
They looked at him and nodded.
They knew just what to do.

Flamingo used her feathers to paint some beads pink.

Zebra rolled on his beads to turn them black and white.

Snake slithered all over her beads, covering them in zig-zags.

Each animal had patterns and colours to give.

Way up above, eagle flew.
He carried some beads up to the sky to turn them blue.
Cheetah came bounding across the plain,
scattering the beads made from his spots.

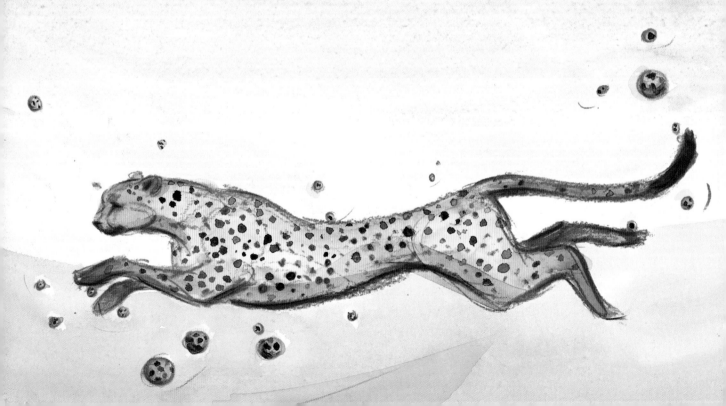

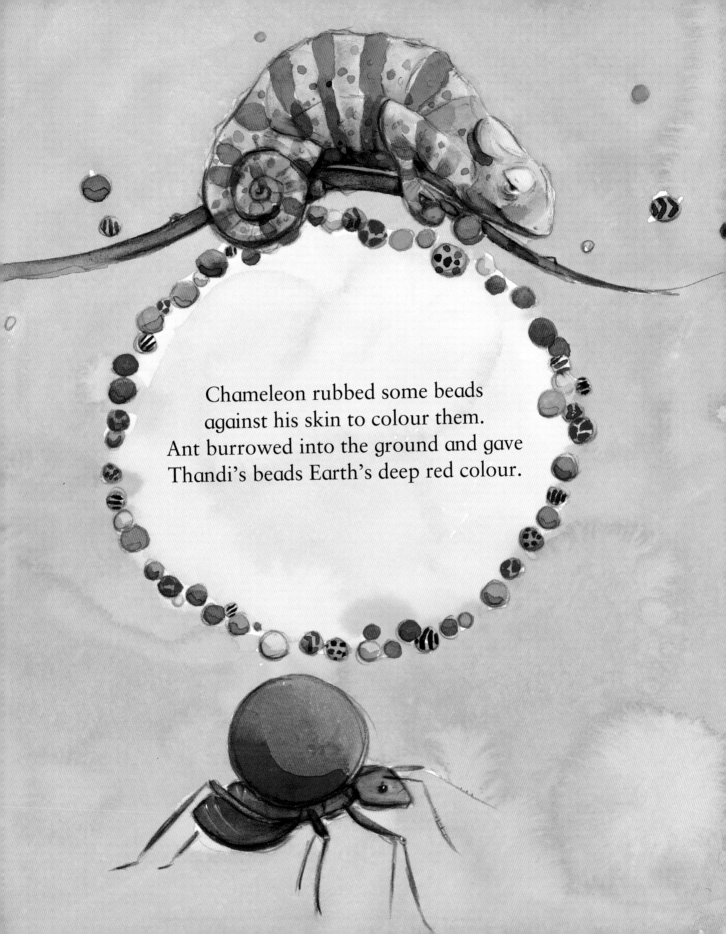

Chameleon rubbed some beads
against his skin to colour them.
Ant burrowed into the ground and gave
Thandi's beads Earth's deep red colour.

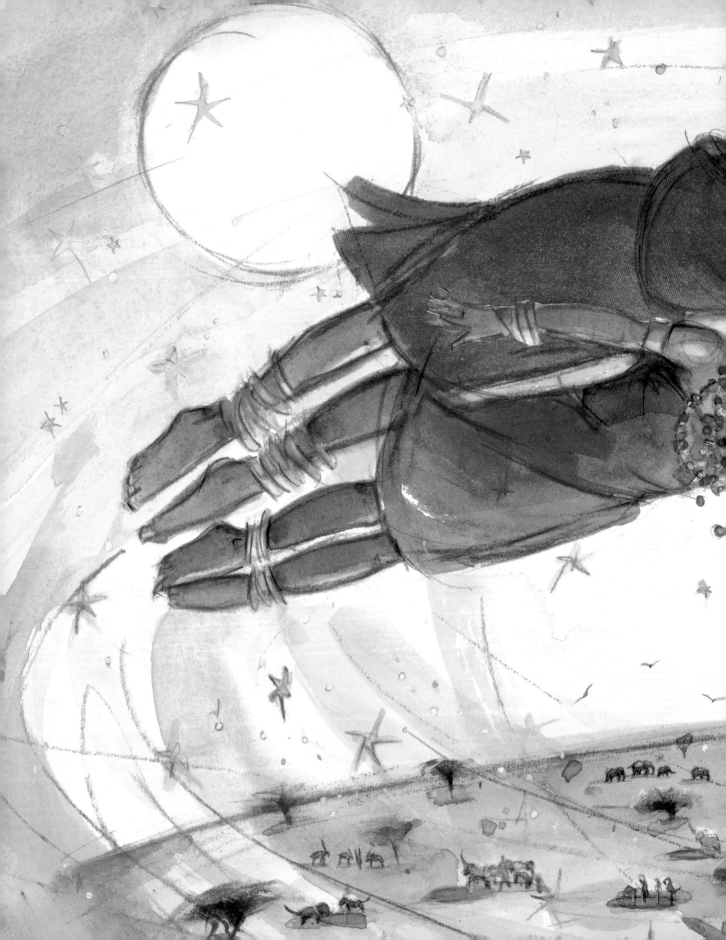

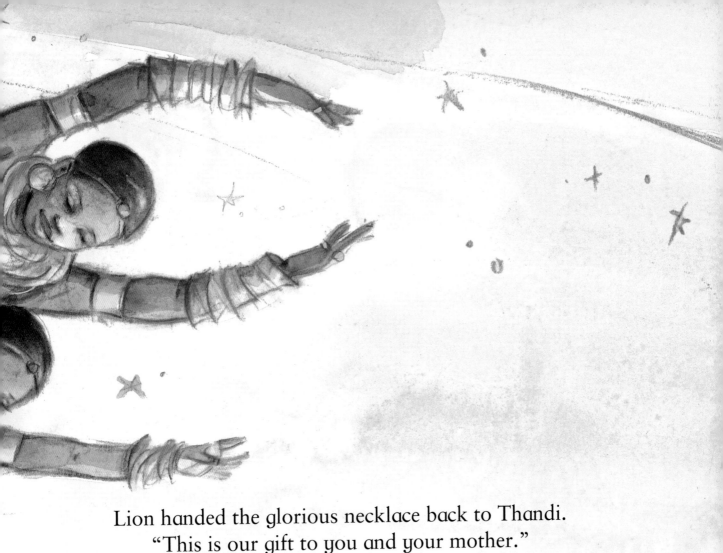

Lion handed the glorious necklace back to Thandi.
"This is our gift to you and your mother."
"Thank you, dear animals, and farewell," said Thandi.
"All is now well on Earth and my work is done," added Lindiwe.
Then, waving goodbye, Lindiwe and Thandi set off,
back to their home in the sky.

Pots

People all over Africa make clay pots as Lindiwe does in the story. They are used to hold water and food. They can also be used for cooking and for ceremonies.

A traditional way of making pots is by rolling clay into long strips. A flat circle of clay is used for the base. Then the strip is coiled round and round on top of it, forming the sides of the pot. The coiled sides are smoothed together and the outside of the pot can be carved or decorated. Then the pot is fired or baked, in the sun or in an oven, to make it hard.

Beads

Today, beads in Africa are often made from glass. But they can also be made from wood, clay or shell.

In many parts of Africa boys and girls wear beads as necklaces, bracelets and anklets. They also use beads as decoration on clothing, shawls and blankets.

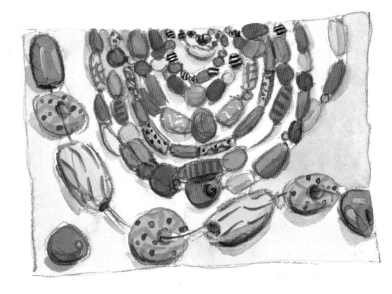

The Dragon Kite

An exciting tale of a daring boy,
his spectacular kite and an
ancient Chinese dragon.

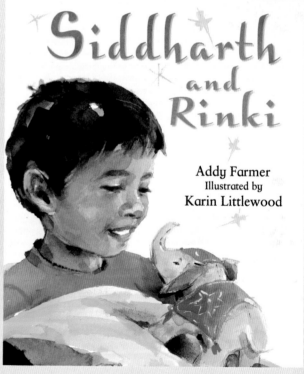

Siddarth and Rinki

A story about a lost toy,
making friends and
getting used to a new life.

OTHER TAMARIND TITLES

Amina and the Shell
The Silence Seeker
The Dragon Kite
Princess Katrina and the Hair Charmer
North American Animals
South African Animals
Caribbean Animals
The Night the Lights Went Out
All My Friends
A Safe Place
Choices, Choices…
What Will I Be?
The Feather
Marty Monster
Starlight
The Bush
Mum's Late
Boots for a Bridesmaid
Yohance and the Dinosaurs

TAMARIND READERS
Reading Between the Lions
Ferris Fleet the Wheelchair Wizard
The Day Ravi Smiled
Hurricane

FOR OLDER READERS, AGED 8–12
Black Stars Series:
David Grant
Rudolph Walker
Benjamin Zephaniah
Malorie Blackman
Lord Taylor of Warwick
Dr Samantha Tross
Jim Brathwaite
Baroness Scotland of Asthal
Chinwe Roy

Barack Obama
Michelle Obama

The Life of Stephen Lawrence
The History of the Steel Band

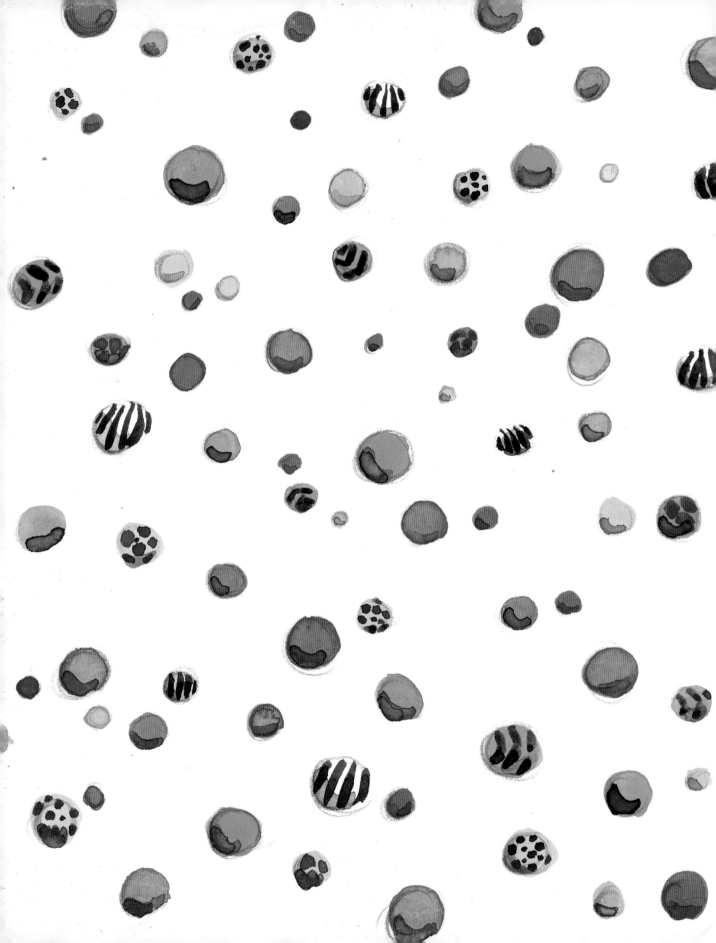